ACCRINGTON STANLEY - Hero of the People!

by Joe Boyle
illustrated by Tony Blundell

First published in Great Britain in Young Lions 1992
3 5 7 9 10 8 6 4 2

Young Lions is an imprint of
HarperCollins Children's Books,
a division of HarperCollins Publishers Ltd,
77–85 Fulham Palace Road,
Hammersmith, London W6 8JB

ISBN 0 00 674376 5

Printed and bound in Great Britain by
HarperCollins Manufacturing, Glasgow

This is Stanley Gawthorp.

He wears round, thick glasses; a
school cap which always slides
over one ear; socks which keep
falling down, and a shirt which
won't stay tucked into his
trousers.

Stanley has never, ever won the Smartest Boy in the World award.

MOST JUNK IN POCKETS

MOST UNUSUAL CACTUS

SMARTEST BOY IN THE WORLD

OLDEST FRUIT GUM

ORST ALLER

LOST MOST DINNER MONEY

SMELLIEST SOCKS

FASTEST WORM

He is very shy and timid, and when people speak to him he blushes so much that his face looks like a hot water bottle.

Now you may think that Stanley looks very much like any other ordinary boy, but he is far from ordinary - and we'll find out why shortly.

First, let's meet Stanley's dad, Herbert.

Herbert Gawthorp owns a tripe
shop, and he and Stanley live
in the flat above. He is plump
and jolly, with a squidgy face
that creases up like a bean bag
when he smiles.

All day long he sits in his tripe
shop, selling tripe and saying
'thank you' to everybody - even
if they don't need thanking.

6

And
this is
Fleabag,
Stanley's
dog.

He enjoys scratching, chasing
cats (though he never catches
any) and singing to the moon.

Chapter One

Stanley, his dad Herbert, and Fleabag have their shop, on a corner, in a pleasant little town called Accrington, which is in the North of England.

But to Stanley, it is the capital of the whole world.

He loves it, and he loves the people who live there.

Accrington folk are so generous.

They help one another through the good times and the bad, in sickness and in health, and every stranger is sure of a cup of tea - even if he doesn't want one.

Every day, in the alley next to
the tripe shop, he would find
things left as presents outside his
door:

bags of garden rubbish,

empty milk bottles,

cardboard boxes,

old three-piece suites,

Stanley just couldn't get over
how generous the folk of
Accrington really were.

Most of the stuff he couldn't find
a use for, but that didn't stop
him from being grateful.

Once he even found a bag of
live kittens, but there were too
many for him to keep, so he had
to give them all away to good
homes.

Stanley often wished that there was some way to repay the kind people of Accrington for their generosity, but he was so timid and shy, and he knew that he would just blush like a big red balloon if they thanked him.

He asked his dad, Herbert, how he might go about it, but Herbert just smiled a squidgy smile and said, 'Thank you'.

Which didn't help at all.

Then, one day, something happened which changed Stanley's whole way of life...

Chapter Two

In a little room at the back of his dad's tripe shop was an old fireplace.

Stanley noticed it one day when he tripped over his shoelace and smacked his nose on the corner. To his amazement, the old fireplace swung open just like a door, and Stanley saw a flight of steps leading down to a cellar.

However, when he
got down there,
he found that
it wasn't a
cellar
at all,

more like a cave,
and oozing out of the
cracks in the walls was
lovely, gooey, grade one tripe.

He had found a tripe mine!

14

(Author's note: this was a most
unusual discovery since tripe is a
kind of food usually found in
butcher's shops.)

There were two reasons why Stanley never told his dad, Herbert, about the secret tripe mine:

1) Herbert would only have smiled a squidgy smile and said 'Thank you'.

2) Stanley discovered that the secret tripe had amazing effects when eaten.

One swallow of the amazing secret tripe was enough to transform timid, shy, Stanley Gawthorp into...

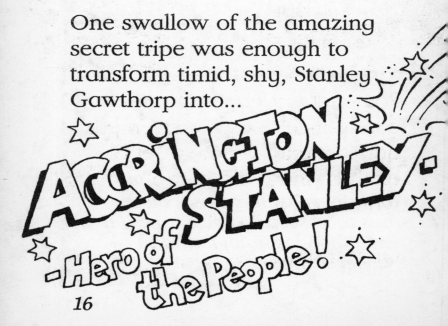

ACCRINGTON STANLEY - Hero of the People!

Somehow, it gave him new
confidence and new strength;
not to mention a new set of
clothes and a cloth cap with 'AS'
written on it.

Quite handy, really.

As Accrington Stanley, he had
no need for his round, thick
glasses, and in his new, striped,
collarless shirt (with
sleeves rolled up)
and his new,
baggy
corduroys
and boots,
he hardly
recognised himself.

Which was great, because now
he would be able to help the
kind folks of Accrington with
their everyday problems of life -
without blushing.

Nobody would know it was him!

Chapter Three

The first thing Stanley did was to fill an old cocoa tin with the secret tripe so that he would never be without any.

The second thing he did was to go out into the High Street and look for good deeds to do.

There was a third thing he knew he must do, but he had forgotten what it was, so he gave Fleabag a bone instead.

It wasn't long before he was surrounded by good deeds he could do.

There were so many, in fact, that he was stuck for choice.

Should he:

1) Help that old lady who was exercising her Rottweiler by running ahead of it, screaming?

2) Offer to carry those sacks for the man in a striped jumper and mask just leaving the bank?

or

3) Return those drinks cans to the gang of skinheads who had just accidentally dropped them?

He just couldn't make up his mind, so he walked on, looking for something which didn't need quite so much thinking about.

It was while he was walking along Hardcastle Street that he heard the sound of sobbing, and saw Mrs Ackroyd weeping into her pinny.

And well she might, for the
washing line which had served
her so well all these years had
suddenly snapped, and there lay
all her newly-washed clothes,
scattered in the mud like pieces
of confetti at a giant's wedding.

'Perfect,' thought Stanley. 'Now's
my chance.'

Chapter Four

Taking the lid off his cocoa tin, he popped a piece of secret tripe into his mouth.

There was a flash, and suddenly, where Stanley Gawthorp had stood one second ago, was...

ACCRINGTON STANLEY - Hero of the People!

Full of daring - not to mention
tripe - and with one eyebrow
raised higher than the other, as
all the best goodies do, he
strode over to where Mrs
Ackroyd stood.

Unfortunately, he had to cross
three gardens to get to her.

And his boots were a little big.

And he didn't have his glasses
on.

He flattened the fence on the
first garden.

Knocked over a greenhouse in
the second garden...

and...

a row of cabbages in the third
garden.

Fleabag contented himself with
chasing a white rabbit which
had hopped out of its pen to see
what the noise was all about.

He didn't know it was a rabbit.
He thought it was a cat with
long ears.

Of course, the house-owners came out and started waving at Stanley, but Stanley decide that now was not the time to give autographs.

'Want some 'elp then, Mrs Ackroyd?' Stanley asked in his most manly voice.

'Oo the 'eck art thee?' said Mrs Ackroyd in her Accrington accent, which, to those who don't live in Accrington, means 'What is your name, young man?'

'I am Accrington Stanley,' said Stanley, 'and I right all wrongs, correct all mistakes, and give 'elp where it is most needed.'

'Well, I'll go t'foot've our stairs!'
gasped Mrs Ackroyd. But what
she really meant was, 'How
remarkable!'

The three house-owners whose gardens Stanley had trampled through, scratched their puzzled heads, and watched as Stanley tried to tie the two ends of the broken washing line together.

They would have liked, very much, to have tied both ends round Stanley's neck.

Stanley found he could make the ends meet, but there just wasn't enough slack to tie them. It began to look as though Accrington Stanley's very first assignment was going to end in failure.

Then an idea hit him

Actually, a clod of earth thrown by one of the house-owners hit him first, but the idea wasn't very far behind.

With amazing swiftness, he took
the string from round the waist
of his baggy corduroy trousers,
and tied it to the two ends of the
washing line.

With equally amazing swiftness,
his baggy corduroy trousers fell
down.

And Mrs Ackroyd's mouth fell
open.

Stanley grabbed the washing
pole and hoisted the mended
line so that the washing could
blow in the wind, after which,
he pulled up his baggy corduroy
trousers.

He thought how pretty the
pattern from his boots looked on
some of the pillowcases.

Mrs Ackroyd was so pleased
that she fainted right away, and
the three house-owners tried
desperately to revive her so that
she could thank Stanley
properly.

But Stanley didn't need thanking.
Besides, he could feel the effects
of the secret tripe wearing off, so
he strode away into the distance,
clutching the waist of his
corduroy trousers, a smile on his
face, and a good job done.

Chapter Five

The news of the escapades of
the town's new hero, Accrington
Stanley, spread rapidly, and
soon his name was on
everybody's lips.

It was a very big name,
however, and those with small
lips had to have it across their
cheeks.

People would gather on street
corners to talk in hushed tones
about his exploits.

Within a week, he had:

1) Re-lit Mrs Rowbotham's gas
when her kettle
went off the boil
for the first time
in twenty years.

2) Rescued Bert Biddle's deaf
        pigeon from the jaws
        of a local tomcat

and

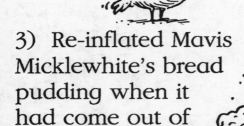

3) Re-inflated Mavis
Micklewhite's bread
pudding when it
had come out of
the oven flat.

Unfortunately, in doing so, he:

1) Blew up Mrs Rowbotham's house.

2) Gave Bert Biddle the cat instead of the pigeon,

and

3) Inflated Mavis Micklewhite's bread pudding with a bicycle pump, so that when she stuck a fork in it, it exploded and blew her wig off.

No wonder the folk of
Accrington were saying things
like:

'Nay!' (Unbelievable!),

'Gerrout!' (Is what
you say true?)

and 'Bloomin' 'eck!'
(My word!).

Chapter Six

It didn't take very long for the news to reach the ears of Gravestone Grimshaw, the roughest, toughest kid in the whole of Accrington.

In fact nothing took very long to reach the ears of Gravestone Grimshaw, especially muck.

He had the biggest ears outside of Chester Zoo.

Some people said that looking at Gravestone Grimshaw was like looking at a taxi with its doors open - but nobody dared say it to his face.

Apart from big ears, Gravestone had a piggy nose, broken teeth, a pointy head, and hair that made him look like he'd had an electric shock.

There was a very good reason why they called him 'Gravestone': when he'd finished bashing you up, you felt you needed one.

Now, over the years, Gravestone had become used to being the centre of attention.

It pleased him when people pointed him out and said, 'There goes Gravestone Grimshaw, the roughest, toughest kid in the whole of Accrington!'

And because he had these big ears, he often heard them say, under their breath '...and the ugliest, and the smelliest...'

Then he'd bash them up, which pleased him even more.

But now, suddenly, no one took any notice of him.

No one pointed him out.

No one talked about him.

Everybody was too busy talking about Accrington Stanley.

And that didn't please him at all!

He scratched his pointy head for three days, which gave him splinters in his fingers and a very good idea for getting rid of Accrington Stanley, for ever.

Chapter Seven

The travelling circus was in town, and Stanley liked animals, so, tucking his cocoa tin containing the secret tripe into his pocket, he set off, with Fleabag who also liked animals, (because he was one) and they soon arrived at the park where the circus was.

There were lots of covered cages
on wheels, and it was by one
covered cage that he came
across a little old lady sobbing
into her handkerchief.

But she was like no other old
lady he had seen before.

She had whopping great ears, a
piggy nose, and her head was
so pointy it pushed her bonnet
up high.

Her voice was different too.

When Stanley asked her why
she was crying, she spoke out of
the side of her mouth and said
in a growly voice, 'Beat it,
Gawthorp!'

Stanley could see she was too
shy to tell him what was wrong,
so he simply slipped behind a
caravan, chewed a little secret
tripe from his cocoa tin, and...
FLASH! ...reappeared as...

The first thing he noticed when
he returned to the little old lady
was that her voice had changed.

It was still growly, but higher.
She explained to him that her
kitten had wandered into the
covered cage and would not
come out no matter how much
she called.

Fleabag's ears sat up. A kitten?
Wasn't that a small cat? Small
cats don't run as fast. Maybe
he'd be able to catch this one.

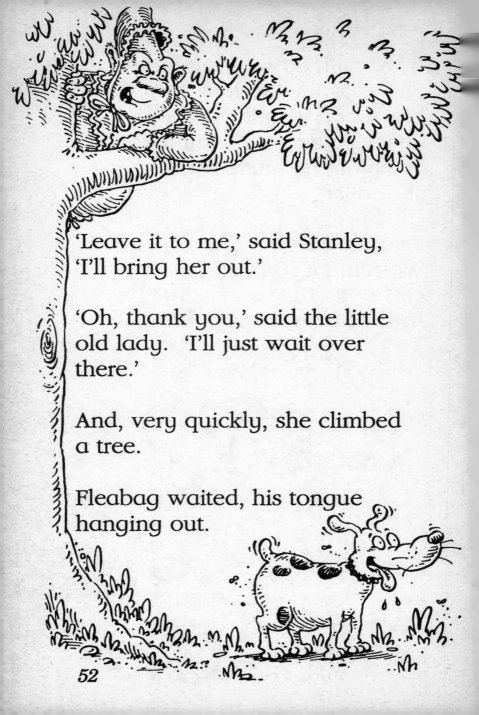

'Leave it to me,' said Stanley, 'I'll bring her out.'

'Oh, thank you,' said the little old lady. 'I'll just wait over there.'

And, very quickly, she climbed a tree.

Fleabag waited, his tongue hanging out.

It was dark inside the cage, but Stanley felt around and soon found what he was looking for.

The kitten purred very, very loudly, and seemed much bigger than the little old lady had led him to believe. In fact, it felt like a very big kitten indeed.

It made such a fuss that the whole cage began to rock, but Stanley took a firm hold on it, and stepped outside into the sunshine.

The first thing Stanley saw was
Fleabag's tail as he vanished
into the bushes.

The little old lady had
disappeared too, but, funnily
enough, all her clothes were in a
pile under the tree.

And there, rolling on the ground
helpless with laughter, was a
figure whom Stanley knew very
well - Gravestone Grimshaw.

'You seen a little old lady
around 'ere, Gravestone?' asked
Stanley, holding on to the bushy
mane of the very big kitten
indeed.

Gravestone had never been
known for his good manners,
so it didn't surprise Stanley in
the least when he made boggly
eyes, screamed, and ran off
without even replying.

Gravestone ran so fast that his
legs looked like a windmill.

He ran so fast that he couldn't
see where he was going.

So he didn't see a tank of hot tar
which workmen were laying on
the road outside the park.

And in he fell - head first!

He bobbed up looking like a
stick of liquorice, hopped out of
the tank, and surprised a
passing van driver so much that
his van skidded and crashed.

The van had been carrying a
load of feathers to the pillow
factory, and suddenly, feathers
were flying everywhere.

Almost every one of them settled
on Gravestone Grimshaw, and
he fled down the road looking
like a chocolate macaroon
on legs.

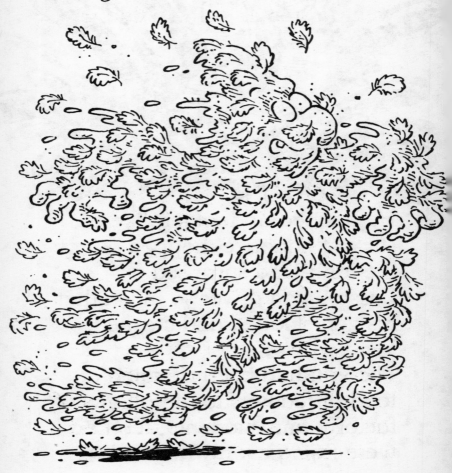

Chapter Eight

Stanley held on tightly to the very big kitten, which wasn't behaving itself very well, and went in search of the little old lady.

Everywhere he looked, people were running. And Stanley thought how very wise it was of the folk in Accrington to spend their time keeping fit like that.

He walked down the High Street - no sign of the little old lady.

No sign of anybody.

'Must be half-day closing,' thought Stanley.

It was taking all his Accrington Stanley strength to stop the very big kitten from running away, and this worried Stanley, because he could feel the effects of the secret tripe wearing off.

Then suddenly...  ...the effects did wear off, and he was plain, timid, Stanley Gawthorp again.

At that very same moment...

Some men threw a net over the very big kitten and carted it away.

The men assured Stanley that it would go to a very good home.

The next day, there was a
picture of Stanley Gawthorp on
the front page of the *Accrington
News*. The story told how he had
captured the escaped lion all by
himself.

Stanley smiled.

Only he knew that it was really a big kitten (the little old lady had said so) and only he knew that it was really Accrington Stanley who had stopped it from running away.

But Stanley wasn't going to say anything. He cut the picture out, pasted it onto a piece of card, and gave it to his dad, Herbert, as a present.

And Herbert smiled his squidgy smile, and said, 'Thank you'.

'Jack sat on the edg[e] [...] move.

"Sit properly Jack, [...] was beginning to s[...]

He shifted along a little. The girl made room [...] him. He turned to speak to her but she had disappeared. He stood up to look for her.

"What's the matter with you, Jack?" the teacher said.

"He's seen the ghost, miss," a boy from the front said and laughed and the whole class began giggling . . .'

Jack doesn't like the look of his new school one bit. And all the children in his class seem really unfriendly. Except one. A lively, mischievous girl in strange old-fashioned clothes, who tells him her name is Jenny. Jack is glad she is there to help him through the first awkward days. But why can nobody else see Jenny?

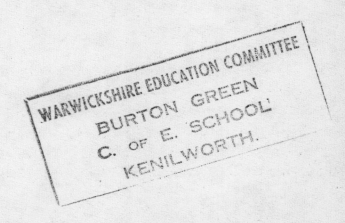

Also by David Wiseman and published by
Corgi Books for older readers:

ADAM'S COMMON
BADGE OF HONOUR

JUMPING JACK
David Wiseman

Illustrated by Jeremy Ford

YEARLING BOOKS

For Daniel and Lucy

JUMPING JACK
A YEARLING BOOK 0 440 862051

Originally published in Great Britain by Blackie and Son Ltd

PRINTING HISTORY
Blackie edition published 1988
Yearling edition published 1989
Reprinted 1990, 1992

This book is set in 14/16 pt Century textbook

Yearling Books are published by Transworld Publishers Ltd.,
61-63 Uxbridge Road, Ealing, London W5 5SA, in Australia by
Transworld Publishers (Australia) Pty. Ltd., 15-23 Helles
Avenue, Moorebank, NSW 2170, and in New Zealand by
Transworld Publishers (N.Z.) Ltd., 3 William Pickering Drive,
Albany, Auckland.

Made and printed in Great Britain by
The Guernsey Press Co. Ltd., Guernsey, Channel Islands

Chapter 1

Jack stood outside his new school.

'It's falling to bits,' he said grumpily. 'And it looks weird.'

'You do talk nonsense,' his mother said.

'Look at it. Look at the date over the door. 1877. It's ancient.'

'There's nothing wrong with that,' his mother said.

'I bet it's haunted. It looks like it to me. And it *is* falling to bits.' He pointed to the roof where a workman was busy replacing some slates.

'Hi!' the workman said when he

saw them. 'You're late. They've all gone in.'

Jack's mother looked up at him. 'This lad of mine thinks the school is haunted.'

The man stopped work and looked down at Jack. 'So it is. I've heard tales. But I've never seen the ghost myself.' He looked hard at Jack and then turned back to his work.

Jack gazed at the building. It was in shadow and looked dark and unfriendly, with windows set high in the stone walls. It was not a bit like his last school which was bright and shiny with glass. That's where all his friends were too, not here.

'Why did we have to move?' he said. But he knew the answer. Dad had to go where the work was, Mam said. He'd been lucky to find a job at all when the factory closed.

'It's not fair,' he grumbled as he followed his mother across the yard.

'Stop nattering,' his mother said. 'This is your school now whether you like it or not. So behave yourself. No fighting.'

He hesitated. He didn't want to go in. He knew the place was haunted. He could tell from the look of it. '1877!' he said and wanted to turn back.

'Come along,' his mother said. 'You'll have to make the best of it. And I expect you'll soon make friends.'

They went into a dimly lit porch and when his mother heard voices she pushed a door open and peered inside.

'Miss Cumberbatch?' she said. A tall, hook-nosed woman, with black wispy hair, came towards them. Jack wondered where she'd left her broomstick.

'Yes?' she said.

'My boy.' Jack's mother pushed him forward. 'Jack Bennett. We've just moved into the village.'

Thirty boys and girls turned their eyes towards him – cold, unfriendly eyes. A boy in the front row made a face and a girl stuck out her tongue. They stared at him as if they hated him. He stared back, hating them. They didn't want him and he didn't want to stay. But there was no escape. His mother had gone and the teacher was standing behind him, her hands on his shoulders.

'This is Jack,' she said. 'He's come to join us so we must make him feel welcome, mustn't we?'

'Yes, miss,' the class said all

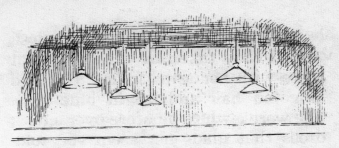

together, but Jack could tell they
didn't mean it.

'There's a desk over there, Jack. Go
and sit down.'

He went to the back of the room.
'Where, miss?' he asked.

The teacher pointed to a desk.
'There.'

9

Jack did not understand. The desk was already taken by a girl. She sat there with her arms folded. She had long fair hair and bright blue eyes. She wore a white pinafore over a dark dress that made her seem very old-fashioned. She looked as if she had been in a fight. She had a scratch down one cheek and her face was streaked with dirt. She smiled at him.

At least she was friendly, not like the rest of them.

'Sit down,' the teacher said.

'But –' Jack began.

'Sit down and let's get on,' she said firmly.

Jack sat on the edge of the seat. The girl didn't move.

'Sit properly Jack,' Miss Cumberbatch said. She was beginning to sound angry.

He shifted along a little. The girl made room for him. He turned to speak to her but she had disappeared. He stood up to look for her.

'What's the matter with you, Jack?' the teacher said.

'He's seen the ghost, miss,' a boy from the front said and laughed and the whole class began giggling.

'Be quiet!' Miss Cumberbatch said and the class stopped laughing, all except the boy at the front. He called, 'Scaredy-cat!'

'Be quiet Roger!' Miss Cumberbatch said again. 'Sit down, Jack, and stop being silly.'

Jack sat down. The girl was there

again, sitting at the desk. Her face broke into a smile.

'Scaredy-cat,' Roger said under his breath. Jack ignored him. He wasn't scared. There was no reason to be.

He looked closely at the girl. There was something strange about her. He wasn't sure what it was. But she was friendly, not like the rest of them. She was even pretty, under the dirt. He smiled at her and she smiled back. He looked away for a moment and when he turned back to her she had gone again. He stood up once more to look for her. 'Will you keep still, Jack!' Miss Cumberbatch exclaimed. 'What is the matter with you? You're like a jumping jack.'

'Jumping Jack, jumping Jack,' the class began to chant until Miss Cumberbatch silenced them. 'You're no better than he is,' she said.

The class settled down to work and the teacher put a piece of paper in front of Jack. 'Tell me all about yourself,' she said. 'Write it all down.

Who you are. Where you've come from.' She rested her hand on his shoulder. 'You'll soon get used to us. You'll soon make friends.'

He didn't believe her. He tried to write but he couldn't. There was nothing to tell, nothing he wanted to tell anyway. He thought of Billy and Joan, the friends he'd left behind at his last school.

'Come on, then,' he heard a whisper in his ear. 'Tell me all about yourself.' The voice was so soft that he thought he must have dreamt it. But he hadn't. It had been real. It was a girl who had spoken, the girl with the dirty face. Who was she? And why did she keep coming and going?

'Come on,' she whispered again. 'Who are you?'

'Jack,' he said. 'Jack Bennett. Who are you?'

'Jenny,' she said. 'Jenny Bryant.'

'Please, miss,' the boy at the next desk said. 'Will you tell the new boy to be quiet? He's talking to himself all the time.'

'Jumping Jack!' someone at the front of the class hissed and the rest of the class began to murmur, 'Jumping Jack, jumping Jack,' until Miss Cumberbatch snapped, 'Behave yourselves!'

'You'll be all right,' Jenny whispered into his ear. 'Don't worry.'

He did not answer, for Miss Cumberbatch was drawing near and she did not look at all pleased. He bent his head and pretended to be busy writing.

Chapter 2

Jack did not want to go out at playtime but Miss Cumberbatch made him. He stood against the school wall watching the other boys and girls playing tig. He looked for Jenny but he couldn't see her anywhere. She was the only one who wanted to make friends. All the others treated him as if he was a creature from outer space. Then one of them, the boy who had pulled a face at him in class, walked up and stood in front of him.

'Who do you think you are?' the boy

said. He sounded as if he wanted a fight, but Jack's mother had told him to be sure to keep out of trouble on his first day.

'What do you want?' he said.

'You're scared,' said the boy.

One of the other boys said, 'Go on, Roger, tell him. Tell him.'

'Tell me what?' Jack said.

'You're daft,' Roger said. 'We all heard you talking to yourself. You're barmy.'

'I don't know what you mean.'

'And you talk funny.' Roger came nearer so that his nose was only a few inches away. Jack wanted to hit it, but he thought he'd better do as his mother said and not get into a fight.

'He's scared, I told you,' Roger said. He raised his fist and shook it in front of Jack's nose. 'See that,' he said. 'Do you want it?'

Jack thrust his hands into his pockets to stop himself hitting out. He heard a whisper in his ear. 'It's all right. You can win.' He knew it was

Jenny. 'I'll help you,' she said. 'I'm not frightened of him,' and, before Jack could stop her, she punched Roger on the nose.

'Ow!' Roger said, put his hand to his nose and yelled 'Ow!' again when he saw blood on his hand.

'What's going on?' Miss Cumberbatch appeared.

'He hit me, miss,' Roger said, snuffling.

'I didn't,' Jack said angrily. 'I never.'

'He did, miss. We saw him, we all saw him. Roger wasn't doing anything and the new boy hit him on the nose.' The crowd shouted, 'It was the new boy, miss.'

'It wasn't, miss, honest,' Jack said, shaking his head.

'If it wasn't you, who was it then?' Miss Cumberbatch said, taking hold of his arm and leading him into school.

'It was –' he began, but he couldn't give Jenny away. He would have hit

Roger himself in another moment, and he wasn't sorry Roger had been hurt.

'You'll have to do better than that if you're to make friends. We can't have fighting. It's no way to behave. I'm sure your mother wouldn't like it.'

Oh no, Jack said to himself, please don't tell Mam. He looked up at the teacher. 'I won't do it again,' he said. 'I promise.'

Miss Cumberbatch smiled. 'That's a good lad. But don't tell lies in future. If you do anything wrong, own up to it. It's easier in the long run.'

He went to his desk and sat down, listening to the noise of the rest of the class playing outside.

'I'm sorry. I didn't mean to get you into trouble,' he heard and saw Jenny standing in front of him.

'You shouldn't be here,' he said. 'Miss Cumberbatch will see you.'

'Oh no she won't,' Jenny said. 'Watch.' She walked over to where the teacher was sitting, picked up the register from the desk and dropped it on the floor. Miss Cumberbatch clicked her tongue in annoyance, picked it up and put it back on the desk but did not say a word to Jenny.

'How did you get away with that?' Jack asked.

Jenny smiled. There was a mischievous look in her eyes and she winked. She went to the front of the classroom again and with a mighty breath blew all the papers from the teacher's desk on to the floor. Miss Cumberbatch, who had gone to the window to keep her eyes on the children in the playground, turned round and looked suspiciously at Jack. But he was sitting at his desk at the back of the room.

She went to the door and made sure it was closed. She shook her head in irritation and picked her papers up, then put a book on them to keep them in place.

'You see,' Jenny said. 'She doesn't know I'm here.'

'Why not?'

'*You* know I'm here. That's all that matters.'

'Where do you live?' he asked. He wanted to meet her after school. It would be good to have a friend to take the place of those he'd left behind.

She didn't answer and he asked again, 'Where do you live?'

'Ah,' she said. 'That would be telling.'

Miss Cumberbatch looked over as if she had heard what they were saying. There was a puzzled look in her eyes as if she found the new boy a very strange case. He smiled at her and she smiled in return, came over and said, 'Do you always talk to yourself?'

'No, miss,' he said indignantly. 'I wasn't.'

'Now, Jack,' Miss Cumberbatch said.

'Be careful,' Jenny whispered in his ear.

'Well sometimes,' he admitted.

'I do, too,' Miss Cumberbatch said. 'Sometimes when I'm on my own.'

She patted Jack on the shoulder and went out to the playground.

'She's not bad, really,' Jenny said. 'But don't tell her about me. She mustn't know. Don't tell anyone.'

'Where do you live?' he asked but she had gone and he felt alone. He still felt alone when the class came in from playtime. They kept turning in their places to look at him, making faces when the teacher wasn't looking and Roger clenched his fist and shook it. Jack ignored him and got on with his work. He kept craning his head to look for Jenny but she was nowhere to be seen.

'Jack Bennett,' Miss Cumberbatch said. 'Will you keep still?'

'Jumping Jack! Jumping Jack!' Roger said and the whole class joined in. Miss Cumberbatch got really angry and threatened to keep them all in after school. 'I want no more of it,' she said.

But at the end of the day when Jack walked up the hill towards home a

group of boys and girls followed him,
calling 'Jumping Jack! Jumping
Jack!' He tried to take no notice but
their taunts were too much for him
and he turned round and faced them.

They stopped and stared at him in
silence. He took a step towards them
and they backed off. He took another
step and another and they turned tail
and ran away. He let them go. He
didn't want a fight. He would keep
out of trouble.

He felt lonely and wanted to make

friends with someone. He wished he knew where Jenny lived. She wanted to be friends. He would ask at the village shop if they knew where Jenny Bryant lived. Someone was bound to know.

Chapter 3

'Well?' Jack's mother said. 'Did you have a good day at school?'

'All right,' he said. He didn't tell her what had happened.

'Did you meet some nice boys and girls? Make any friends?'

'They're all right,' he said. 'There was one girl who was friendly.' He hadn't meant to tell his mother about Jenny. He'd meant to keep the news of her to himself as Jenny had asked him to.

Luckily his mother didn't ask him any more. She was too busy getting dinner for the family.

'You can peel some potatoes for me,' she said. 'We've all got a lot to do.'

The house was still in a mess after the move, with boxes still unpacked, furniture still not in its proper place. His father and mother said they had to do a lot of repairs on the old cottage before it was really fit for them.

'And don't get under my feet,' his mother said. 'When you've finished the potatoes you can go for a walk. I expect there's lots to explore.'

He was good at peeling potatoes and had soon finished. He did as his mother told him and got out from under her feet and went to explore. He went along the lane wondering where it led. Once, long ago, there had been a lot of mines near here, where men had dug for tin and copper. Perhaps the lane led to mine workings. That would be something worth exploring. There might even be other metals besides tin and copper, perhaps gold.

He went on, until he saw a huge building in front of him. It was half in ruins, with a tall chimney at one corner. Ivy clung to the walls and jackdaws fluttered about the gaping windows.

Jack walked towards the ruin.

'Hey! Boy!' a shout came and he saw a man leaning over a gate waving a stick at him. 'Come here, boy!'

He wondered what he'd done wrong. He didn't move.

'I won't bite, boy. You come along here now. You don't want to wander over there. It's not safe. There are old men's workings here and there, everywhere.'

'Old men's workings?'

'Holes in the ground, boy, fathoms deep. Old mine shafts. It's dangerous hereabouts.'

Jack walked over to him. 'I didn't know,' he said.

'I can see that,' said the man. 'You're a stranger here?'

'We've just moved in,' Jack explained.

'Oh yes,' the man said. 'You'll be living at Rose Cottage.'

'What's that old building?' Jack asked.

'It's an engine house. Empty now,

but used to hold the engine that pumped water from the mines to stop them flooding.' He shook his finger at Jack. 'You be careful, boy. The moors round about are riddled with shafts. Watch where you go.' He turned away and walked off across the fields shaking his head.

Jack went back home along the lane. He didn't know whether to believe the man or not, but he'd done enough exploring for the day. He was feeling hungry and as he drew near the cottage an appetizing smell made his mouth water. In spite of all the work his mother had to do on the house she was still the best cook in the world.

His father carried a large brown pot, steaming with goodness, on to the table. His brother Harry and sister Roberta, who were at secondary school, claimed they had too much homework to have time to help. They sat and waited to be served. Jack thought they were lazy. He was always the one to be told to lay the table and help with the washing-up. He screwed up his face at them when they asked him how he'd got on at school.

'You got into trouble, I suppose,' Harry said.

'Trust you,' said Roberta.

He ignored them. They were always teasing him.

'Leave him alone,' his father said. 'You two are no angels either.'

'He's made a friend already,' his mother said as she sat down. 'Haven't you, Jack?'

He didn't answer. He'd promised Jenny not to tell anyone about her.

'Ah ha!' said Roberta. 'It's a girl, I can tell. He's blushing.'

'Get on with your dinner,' Mr Bennett said. 'And leave the boy alone.' He grinned at Jack and winked as if he knew all about the friend he was keeping to himself. Perhaps I can tell Dad, Jack thought, and then knew he must not break his word to Jenny. Jenny was a secret – his secret.

Chapter 4

Jenny was waiting in the playground for him when he got to school the next day. It was good to see a friendly face. No one else smiled at him but Jenny came over and said softly, 'It will be all right. Don't worry.'

He had been worried. He did not want to come here. He wanted to go back to his old school where his friends were. Without Jenny this place would be horrid.

Roger Marshall, the boy who had tried to pick a fight, scowled at him. He kept his distance but called,

'Jumping Jack, jumping Jack, fell down a shaft and broke his back.'

Then the whole school took up the chant. Jack faced them but he did not know what to do. 'I hate them,' he said to himself. 'I hate them all. Except Jenny,' he added.

She whispered to him, 'Shall I teach him a lesson?' And before Jack could answer she left his side and walked towards the crowd.

Roger was jeering and chanting. Suddenly he fell flat on his face and the noise stopped.

'There,' said Jenny, coming back to Jack. 'Serve him right.'

Roger got to his feet, looked round and started arguing with one of his friends. 'You pushed me,' he said and hit out.

'I didn't,' his friend denied, but hit back at Roger, and soon the two of them were rolling on the floor, snapping and snarling at each other like angry cats.

Miss Cumberbatch appeared. 'Get

up,' she said. 'I don't know what's come over you.' Jenny sniggered and Jack said, 'Shut up. You'll get into trouble.'

Miss Cumberbatch looked at him sharply. 'Did you say something, Jack Bennett?'

'No, miss,' he answered.

The morning passed quietly except that every now and again Jenny would leave her place and wander round the room. Jack did not know how she dared and he wondered why Miss Cumberbatch said nothing to stop her. When Jenny tipped Roger's books on to the floor the teacher blamed Roger for it.

When Jenny came back Jack whispered, 'Why did you do that?' Jenny winked and raised her eyebrows. Jack said 'You'll get into trouble.' He could see Jenny was planning more mischief.

He could not understand why Jenny was allowed to get away with such naughtiness. Why did Miss Cumberbatch say nothing and why did the other boys and girls pay no attention to her?

'Who are you?' he said. 'Where do you come from?'

'Please, miss,' Walter Jones, the boy in the next desk, complained. 'Will you stop the new boy talking? He's getting on my nerves.'

Jack was cross. 'I wasn't talking to you.'

Miss Cumberbatch looked at him. 'Well, Jack?' she said. How could he explain without giving Jenny away?

'I'm sorry, miss,' he said.

There were times when Jenny disappeared altogether. He missed her then but was able to get on with his work.

He was writing about himself, for Miss Cumberbatch. 'At my last school I had two good freinds,' he wrote.

Jenny appeared and said. 'You spelt that wrong.'

'I didn't,' he protested.

'It's f,r,i,e,n,d,' she said, spelling

the word out. ' "I before e except after
c." '

He corrected the spelling. Jenny
wandered off again. He hoped she
would not do anything silly, but the
look in her eye showed she was feeling
impish. He bent to his work then
looked up at a cry of annoyance from
Miss Cumberbatch. The blackboard
duster was waving in the air in front
of her, scattering clouds of chalk dust
in the air. Miss Cumberbatch sneezed,
a gale of a sneeze, a hurricane, a
tempest. The papers on her desk went
flying in a gust of 'Attishoos'.

'Bless my soul!' Miss Cumberbatch
said when she stopped. 'What's going
on here?' She looked around to see
who to blame but the class all looked
as surprised as she was. Except
perhaps the new boy.

'Jack,' she began but Jack hadn't
left his seat. He could not have done
anything.

But when it was time for play, she
told Jack to stay in school. 'Help me

tidy up,' she said. And he willingly did as he was told.

He knew Jenny was not far away. He could hear her whistling 'Pop Goes the Weasel' to herself. He thought she was hiding in a cupboard but when he opened it there was no sign of her. Then he looked for her behind the teacher's desk.

'Jack,' said Miss Cumberbatch. 'What are you doing? I have never met such a restless boy.' She left him to finish while she went into the playground. When she had gone he called 'Jenny, Jenny.' But no one answered. He saw the class register on the teacher's desk and thought he would find out where Jenny lived. He opened it and read the names. His was the last, of course, and his address, Rose Cottage. But there was no Jenny Bryant, no Jenny at all. She did not belong to the class.

Then what was she doing here? 'Jenny!' he called again and knew she was near. He couldn't see her, but he knew she was beside him. 'Jenny,' he said. 'Who are you?'

But he knew now, without asking. He guessed he had known all along. The school *was* haunted – by Jenny. She was real to him but no one else saw her: not Miss Cumberbatch, not the other boys and girls. She wasn't real to them. She could not be a real live person because no one else seemed to see her.

She was a ghost. A ghost who showed herself only to him.

Jenny, a ghost? He could not believe it. How could a ghost correct his spelling? Or hit Roger Marshall on the nose?

And ghosts were frightening. But he wasn't frightened of Jenny. She had made friends with him. She liked him. And he liked her.

'Jenny,' he called again softly. And she was there, looking at him with those big eyes, full of mischief, smiling, laughing eyes. 'Who are you?' he said.

'You know,' she said. 'Jenny Bryant.'

'Why does no one else know you are here?'

'You know I'm here. That's all that matters.'

And he thought, yes, that's all that matters.

Chapter 5

Jack wished Jenny would appear at home as well as at school, even if she was a ghost. He wanted to tell some-one about her but knew he couldn't. His brother and sister would laugh at him, say he was imagining things. His mother would be worried about him

There *was* nothing to worry about. Jenny would do him no harm. She was his friend, the only one he had here.

She did not show herself at home. So he was on his own. Harry and Roberta were not interested in the same things as him. His mother and

39

father were so busy working on the cottage that he was left to himself.

On the Saturday morning his parents were joined by the workman who had been on the school roof. He greeted Jack cheerfully. 'Seen any ghosts?' He laughed loudly. 'Made friends yet?' he asked. 'They're a funny lot but they're all right. You'll soon get to know them.' He was helping Jack's Dad take out an ugly tiled fireplace and was covered in dust. 'My lad's there, Roger, Roger Marshall. D'you know him? I expect you do.'

Oh yes, I know him, Jack said to himself.

'I'll tell him to come and see you.'

Don't bother, thought Jack, but he kept it to himself. Mr Marshall was friendly enough, but Roger wasn't.

'I'm going for a walk, Mam,' he called.

'Watch where you go,' Mr Marshall said. 'It's dangerous round about here. Keep to the paths. Don't wander off over the Downs. It looks safe enough, but there are shafts all over the place. Last year the local hunt went after a fox there. The old fox was wiser than they were. He knew all the twists and turns. Knew where the old workings were. The hounds didn't. They tumbled down a deep shaft. And all but three were lost.'

'Is that true?' Jack's mother asked.

'Oh certain sure. They won't ever hunt over this ground again. So, watch it, young Jack. Be careful. Keep to the proper paths.'

Jack kept to the paths, though he was tempted to wander. The Downs were covered with purple heather and yellow gorse. The sky was blue and even the ruined buildings looked beautiful.

He saw a movement in the heather and thought it was a rabbit. He went to look more closely and heard a sudden whisper, 'No. No.' He thought he felt a hand dragging him back on to the path. 'You mustn't,' he heard but he could not see her. He knew it was

Jenny, but she sounded frightened, tearful. 'No, please,' she said. 'Please don't.'

He stepped back on to the path and heard a sigh of relief.

'Jenny,' he called. 'Jenny. Where are you?' But there was no answer. Jenny was no longer with him. He felt alone. He called again, but it was no use.

When he got back home he found his parents and Mr Marshall excited at what they had found when they removed the fireplace. Behind it they had discovered a huge stone hearth and a small clay oven off one side.

'It's an old house, all right,' said Mr Marshall. 'And look what else we found.' He held up some sheets of paper. 'A newspaper, over a hundred years old, I reckon.'

'Give it to me,' said Jack's mother. 'Dirty old thing.' She was going to throw it away but Jack begged her to let him have it.

'Take it outside, then, and get rid

of the dust.'

He took it to the back door and blew the dust off it, but it was still very sooty. He could just make out the date. Mr Marshall was right. It *was* over a hundred years old. 'April 17, 1878' he read with difficulty.

He took the paper up to his room. It was very brittle and he had to handle it very carefully or it would crumble into pieces.

'Dinner time,' he heard his mother call and rushed downstairs. His walk over the Downs had made him hungry.

'Look at your hands,' his mother said. They were covered with soot. He hurried to wash them and came back quickly, mouth watering at the smell of dinner.

'I don't know how you manage it, love,' his dad said to his mother. 'All this going on around you and you still manage to feed us like this.'

She was the best cook in the world, Jack thought, as he began to eat.

Chapter 6

He knew now that Jenny was a ghost. It made no difference. He liked her and looked forward to seeing her at school. When he did not see her he hoped she wasn't ill. But he didn't suppose ghosts could get ill.

Roger was there in the playground. Perhaps he should go up and say hello, but he didn't see why he should.

Two of the boys began to whisper together. Then they raised their voices. 'Jumping Jack, jumping Jack, fell down a shaft and broke his back.' Soon everyone was chanting, except

Roger. He turned on the others, said something and they stopped.

When they went into school Jenny was there, sitting in Jack's place. He joined her. It was funny the way he could sit there and know that Jenny was there too, not taking up any room, but there all the same. He said, 'Hello.' She winked and whispered, 'Watch!'

He watched her. She went to the teacher's desk, took the class register and hid it under the cushion on Miss Cumberbatch's chair. Miss Cumberbatch sat down and looked on the desk for the register. It wasn't there. She searched among her papers, then on the floor. She stood up, went round the classroom, came back to her desk and sat down again. She opened all the drawers once, twice and three times.

'Has anyone seen the register?' she asked.

No one spoke. Jack felt guilty and half raised his hand.

'Don't!' Jenny said. He could tell she was laughing.

'Well?' Miss Cumberbatch said. 'Do you know something, Jack?'

'Don't you dare!' Jenny said into his ear.

'No, miss,' Jack said.

'I expect it'll turn up,' the teacher said, but she looked at Jack as if he might know more than he said. He whispered to Jenny out of the side of his mouth, 'You'll get me into trouble.'

'He's at it again,' said Walter Jones. 'The new boy's talking to himself, miss.'

'He's not the new boy,' Miss Cumberbatch said. 'He's got a name. It's Jack.'

'Jumping Jack,' hissed a girl.

Miss Cumberbatch looked daggers at her, and Jenny walked over and pulled the girl's plait.

'Ow!' she yelled and turned round and slapped the face of the boy behind her. He grabbed her arm and they fell to the floor. Miss Cumberbatch said sternly, 'I've had quite enough of this. I really don't know what's got into you all. You used to be so well-behaved.' She looked at Jack again as if it was his fault.

He wanted to explain but no one would believe him. He spoke to Jenny as quietly as he could. 'You'd better stop. It's not funny.'

'I'll stop when they stop teasing you,' she said. He wanted to tell her he could stand up for himself, but she only meant to help and he didn't want to upset her. Even if she was a ghost she was the only real friend he had and he was glad she was there.

'Ah!' said Miss Cumberbatch when she went back to her desk. 'There it is.' The register was open in front of her, as if it had been there all the time. She shook her head as if she could not understand what was going on.

At playtime Jenny did not follow Jack into the yard but he felt she was watching and listening, ready to help him.

Roger Marshall came near but did not speak.

Jack thought if he wants to make friends, he'll have to speak first. I'm not bothered.

But he was bothered. He wanted to be friends. He turned to Roger and said, 'I'm sorry I made your nose bleed.' He hadn't done it, but Roger wouldn't believe that.

'That's all right,' said Roger. 'You just took me by surprise.'

They went into school and got on with their work. Jenny was quiet and well-behaved, even helping Jack with his sums, pointing out when he made a mistake. She was always right.

He wanted to know more about her, but he did not dare speak for Walter Jones was ready to complain. So he took a piece of paper and wrote, 'Where do you come from?'

'Me?' he heard Jenny say. He nodded.

'Somewhere.'

'Why are you here?' he wrote.

'Don't you like me?' she whispered.

'Of course I like you,' he wrote and realized the teacher was standing by him.

'What are you writing?' she asked.

Before he could reply Jenny

snatched the paper from the desk, tore it into little pieces and threw them in the air.

The scraps floated about the room, caught by a breeze, fluttering here and there. Jack could hear Jenny laughing, a tinkling laugh, full of mischief.

'Jack,' Miss Cumberbatch said. 'I think we'd better have a talk.'

So, at lunch-time, she sat Jack in front of her and talked. She wanted to know all about him, what his last school was like, who his friends were, and what he liked doing.

He tried to answer her truthfully. But he knew she wanted to know about Jenny. And he would tell her nothing about that. Jenny trusted him to keep her secret.

'Ah well,' Miss Cumberbatch sighed. 'If that's all you want to tell me, off you go.' He was relieved. He might have told her about Jenny if she had gone on a bit longer. She was quite nice really.

He wanted to know about Jenny

51

too but she would tell him nothing. He thought someone in the village might know about her. He went to the village shop and said he was looking for a family called Bryant. They could tell him nothing.

'There's no one of that name. We'd know all right.' The shopkeeper turned to his wife. 'Have you heard of anyone called Bryant?'

His wife looked at Jack with interest. 'You've just moved into Rose Cottage, haven't you?'

Jack nodded.

'No,' she said. 'I don't know anyone called Bryant, but old Mrs Pascoe at the farm might. She goes back a long way. She's almost a hundred years old. She knows everyone who's ever lived here. Ask her.'

But he felt too shy to go to the farm. He'd never met anyone as old as that and wouldn't know what to say. He went home with his questions about Jenny still unanswered.

Chapter 7

At last he plucked up enough courage
to go to see Mrs Pascoe.

When he knocked on the door he
wondered what he could say. When no
one came he was glad and turned to
leave.

'Hello! What do you want?' He
turned to see an old woman kneeling
beside a flower bed. 'Now you're here
you can give me a hand with these
weeds.' She pointed to a heap of
dandelions she had collected. 'There's
plenty more. Get a move on.'

He bent down and started to pick

the weeds. He glanced at her out of
the corner of his eye. She was small
and very thin, her face full of wrinkles
but her eyes were bright.

'Well,' she said. 'What do you think
of me?'

He blushed. He hadn't meant her to
see he was curious about her.

'Lost your tongue?'

He shook his head.

'Help me up,' she said. He put his
hand out and she gripped it with thin
claw-like fingers and got to her feet.
'Can you hear the creaks?' she said.

'That's my bones. They need oiling. You can put the kettle on for me and we'll have a cup of tea.'

He followed her into the house and did as she told him, made the tea and poured it for them. 'Sit down,' she ordered and again he did as he was told.

'So,' she said. 'You're the new boy.'

'I'm Jack Bennett,' he said.

'I know all about you.' She dipped a biscuit into her tea and then sucked it noisily. 'And what do you want calling on an old thing like me?'

'I –' he began.

'Go on. I'm waiting. I won't bite.' She cackled. 'My old teeth wouldn't manage a tough young thing like you.'

He did not know what to say.

'You are tough, are you?' She took a pair of steel-rimmed glasses from her pocket and perched them on her nose. She peered at him through them. 'Yes,' she said, 'you're tough.' She took the glasses off, put them back in her pocket and sipped her biscuit again. She was silent for a long time and he thought she had gone to sleep. But suddenly she said, 'And how do you like your new school? It's haunted. Did you know?'

He nodded.

'Have you seen her?' she asked.

He gulped. Perhaps he could tell the old lady. He was sure he could trust *her*.

'She's a good sort. She won't do you any harm,' the old lady said.

'Have *you* seen her?' he asked, but she had gone quiet again. Her eyes were closed. Her skin was brown and wrinkled like a walnut shell. He got up quietly, so as not to wake her.

'Where are you off to?' she said sharply.

He sat down again and waited.

'Ninety years ago, I was your age. How old are you?'

'Nine.'

'I was nine when I came here. Went to school and didn't know a soul.

Didn't like them, except her.'

'Jenny,' he said.

'So you *have* seen her. Spoken to her, I expect.'

He nodded. 'What do you know about her?' he asked.

The old woman sighed. 'I could never find anything out. But she was kind. Wicked too. Always up to mischief. Got me into trouble quite a lot. And then one day she went. I never saw her again. I'd made other friends by then. They've all gone now.' She closed her eyes again but Jack did not think she had gone to sleep. He waited. 'Tell Jenny I think of her. Tell her Millie remembers her. That's my name, you see, not just Mrs Pascoe but Millie. Nobody calls me by my name now but Jenny will remember.'

'I'll tell her,' he said.

He was no nearer knowing all about Jenny, but he knew now she was real, at least as real as a ghost could be. Mrs Pascoe had seen her too. Millie – he must tell Jenny about her.

Chapter 8

'I met someone you know,' he whispered to Jenny.

She did not seem to be interested.

'An old lady called Millie,' he said.

'I don't know any old ladies.'

'She wasn't old when she met you. She was only nine. It was a long time ago.'

'Please, miss. He's talking to himself again,' Walter Jones complained.

Jack pretended to be busy at his work. He was never able to talk to Jenny. He could never ask her about herself. He would have to try to get her on her own. But he never could.

He would have to come back to school when there was no one else there.

At playtime he asked Miss Cumberbatch if he could stay in. She said, 'No. You need fresh air.' He went out with the rest of the class. He hoped Jenny would come out too but she stayed behind. Roger spoke to him, but he did not want to make friends, not yet. It was Jenny he was interested in.

At the end of the afternoon he whispered to Jenny, 'I'm coming back when everyone has gone. I'll come to meet you.'

'No,' she said quickly. 'No, please don't.'

'Yes,' he said. 'I want to talk to you.'

'Please don't,' she said. 'You mustn't.'

Miss Cumberbatch was watching and he had to leave. But he had made his mind up. He would come back. He was determined to find out all he could about Jenny, why she was there in school, what had happened to her.

He went home and had tea. When he had finished he told his mother he was going for a walk.

'Going to meet a friend?' she said.

'Yes,' he said. He didn't tell her what sort of friend. She would think he was off his head. Perhaps he was, but then if *he* was, so was old Mrs Pascoe.

The school was silent. He stood outside for a few minutes to make sure the caretaker had gone. Then he went to the back of the school to find a way in.

He heard a sudden flutter of sound and jumped. It was a jackdaw in the bell tower. It watched him, head perched on one side. It seemed to know he should not be there.

He heard voices inside the school and stood close into the wall to hide. Miss Cumberbatch was talking to Mrs Williams, the caretaker.

'Have you heard the story that the school is haunted? It's nonsense of course,' the teacher said.

'It's no nonsense,' Mrs Williams said. 'I've heard a young maid has been seen. A poor sad little thing.'

That's not my ghost, thought Jack.

Jenny isn't sad. She's always cheerful, full of fun and wickedness.

The voices faded and in a moment he heard footsteps in the school yard. He crept to the corner and watched Miss Cumberbatch and Mrs Williams walking away together.

He tried the back door, but it was bolted. He clambered up to a window and that was locked. He slipped down and grazed his knuckles. He tried every window and they were all fastened. He was afraid he would be seen if he went to the front of the school. But there was no way in at the back.

He peered round the corner of the building. No one was in sight. He ran up the steps to the front door and tried it. It opened. He could not believe it. But it opened.

He slipped in quickly and closed the door behind him. The school felt strange, not empty as it should. He was being watched, he was sure. Lots of eyes followed his every move, though he could not see them. He could hear breathing and he stopped, afraid.

It was his own breathing. He was afraid of himself. He should not be here. If anyone came he would tell them he had left his school bag behind.

He stood in the porch, not daring to move. There was rustling all around him, in every corner. Perhaps mice lived here when the boys and girls had gone. Perhaps they sat at the desks with a mouse teacher learning how to trick the cats. The idea cheered him up a little, but only a little.

He wished now he had not come.

And where was Jenny? He called, 'Jenny,' softly, not wanting to disturb the mice too much. There was no answer. He called again but he heard only the echo of his own voice, 'Jenny! Jenny!'

It was dark inside school but he did not dare to switch the light on. He fumbled his way to the door of his classroom. Jenny would be there. Then at last he could talk to her freely, without Walter Jones eavesdropping.

The door groaned as he pushed at it. He had not noticed that before and it made him jump. He pushed it wider and stepped inside.

The room felt cold and it looked odd in the half-light. There was a hush about it. There were no more rustlings. There were no mice sitting at the desks, no mouse teacher at the front.

The room was filled with long wooden benches. An old-fashioned high teacher's desk was at the front. He could just make it out in the gloom. He stood at the door, surprised at what he saw. He called softly again, 'Jenny! Jenny!'

There was no answer.

'Jenny. Where are you? I've come to talk.'

Silence.

But she was here. He knew.

'Please,' he said. 'Please say something.'

There was a long sigh, but nothing more.

He took a step into the room,
another and another. And stopped.

On one of the benches something
was stretched out, a bundle of blankets, he thought.

He went slowly to it and put out a hand to touch it. There was something under the blankets, some body.

He had to know.

He lifted the end of the blanket and pulled it slowly back.

It was Jenny lying there, eyes closed, face pale under the dirt, a streak of blood on her cheek.

It was Jenny and she did not speak. She could not. It was not the live ghost he was seeing. It was her dead body.

He was not afraid, but he felt a sadness creeping over him. He reached out to touch her hair, to smooth it away from her face. As he did, the door behind him opened and light shone in.

'What are you doing here?' It was the caretaker, Mrs Williams.

He blinked. The benches had gone. The room was as always, desks tidily arranged, with the chairs lifted on top of them for easy cleaning.

'What are you doing here?' Mrs

Williams repeated. 'How did you get in?'

He gulped, unable to forget what he had seen.

'Well?' she said.

'I . . . I came to look for my school bag,' he said.

'Did you find it?' She stared at him. 'Are you all right? You look as if you've seen a ghost.'

'I'm all right,' he said.

'It's a good job I looked in before locking up. You'd have been here all night otherwise.'

He was glad she chattered on. It helped him to forget what he had seen.

He could not forget. And he knew now why Jenny had not wanted him to come back to school. She must have known what he would find.

'Jenny,' he said softly as he left the building, 'see you on Monday.'

But would he? What had happened to her?

Chapter 9

'Did you meet your friend?' Jack's mother asked him.

He did not answer. He did not know what to say.

'It's a girl,' his brother Harry said. 'You can tell.'

'Don't tease him,' his mother said. 'Why shouldn't he make friends with a girl?' She smiled at him so that he wanted to tell her about Jenny. But even his mother would not understand. Only Mrs Pascoe would.

The next day, Saturday, Mr Marshall again came to help with the work on the house. He brought his son Roger with him.

'You two ought to make friends,' he said. 'Perhaps you can keep each other out of trouble.'

Jack's father laughed. 'It usually works the other way.'

Jack looked at Roger and Roger looked at Jack.

'Well?' said Mr Marshall. 'Have you nothing to say to each other?'

'Come on,' said Roger. 'Let's get away from here.'

'Don't go over the Downs,' Mr Marshall shouted after them. 'I've warned you about that. It's not safe.'

Roger and Jack walked along the lane until they came to the path leading over the Downs. Roger said, 'I don't know why he makes such a fuss. I know my way about.' He stepped off the path and made his way through the clumps of heather to a heap of rocks.

'Come on,' he said. 'You're not frightened, are you?'

Jack went cautiously across to Roger. 'I collect rocks,' Roger said. 'I've got all sorts. I know just where to look.'

'Your dad said it's not safe,' Jack said.

'I know what I'm doing,' Roger said. He searched among the stones but did not find anything of interest. 'I often come here,' he said. 'Don't tell Dad. He'd skin me if he knew.'

'I'm sorry I made your nose bleed,' Jack said. 'Only you seemed to want a fight.'

'Well, you were a new boy,' Roger said, as if that was enough excuse. 'Anyway they won't call you Jumping Jack any more. I've told them what I will do if they start that again.'

'I don't mind,' Jack said. But he did really and he was glad Roger had told the others to stop. He bent down and began to search among the rocks, picking pieces of stone up and asking his friend about them. Roger seemed to know a lot, or pretended to.

He pointed to a squat ruined building. 'There are some good stones
there, in the old clock tower. Want to
come?'

'Not now,' said Jack. 'It's time for
dinner.'

They went back. Jack's mother had
made dinner for them all, Mr Marshall
and Roger as well. He was glad Roger
would see what a good cook his mother
was. He was glad Roger had become
his friend. Now he had two friends,
Roger and Jenny. It was a pity he

couldn't tell Roger about Jenny, but he had promised her.

Back at school on Monday Miss Cumberbatch asked him if he had found his school bag. 'It was at home all the time,' he said, but he felt guilty about lying to her.

He looked around for Jenny, but she was not to be seen. He got down to work, expecting her to appear and help him with his sums. But there was no sign of her. He did not dare to call her name in case Walter Jones told the teacher.

At playtime he joined Roger and soon was playing with the others as if he had known them all his life. No one chanted after him. He was happy. It wasn't such a bad school after all. He even forgot to look for Jenny but, when he left school in the afternoon and passed the farm, he remembered her and decided to call on Mrs Pascoe. Perhaps she had thought of something else. Perhaps he could tell her what he had seen.

When he knocked at the farmhouse door it was not Mrs Pascoe who opened to him, but another woman.

'I'm sorry,' she said. 'Mrs Pascoe isn't well enough to see anyone.' She closed the door before he could ask when he might come back.

He went home disappointed, still wanting to know about Jenny, wanting to ask her to explain things.

But there was no sign of her, not that day, nor at any time. As the weeks went by and she did not show herself he stopped thinking of her. He went to see Roger's collection of rocks and Roger gave him one or two stones so he could start a collection too.

Once or twice he dreamt about Jenny, but soon he began to think he had imagined it all. After all there were no such things as ghosts. Everyone said so.

Except Mrs Pascoe, he remembered.

Chapter 10

Roger promised to help Jack find some rocks for his collection. They agreed to meet after tea. The evenings were light now and Jack looked forward to the search.

He was still uneasy about wandering over the Downs. But Roger seemed to know his way about. Jack did not tell his mother where he was going. She would not approve.

'I'm going for a walk,' he said. 'I'm going to meet Roger.'

'Help me to mix this wallpaper paste first,' she said. Jack's Dad was getting ready to paper the sitting room.

'I'll be late,' Jack said but he stayed to stir the paste until his mother was satisfied.

'The house will soon be finished,' she said. Jack thought it would never be finished. There was always something more to do.

He ran along the lane. He *was* late. He had arranged to meet Roger by the old engine house, on the edge of the Downs.

There was no sign of his friend. Perhaps he had got fed up with waiting and had gone home. Or perhaps he had gone over the Downs by himself. But Jack could not see him. He called his name, but there was no answer.

Jack hesitated, stepped off the path and began to walk across the heather. But he did not feel safe. Roger knew his way about, but he didn't.

He went back to the engine house and waited. After a while he decided to go back home. He was disappointed,

but there would be other days. He was surprised Roger had not waited for him. He called his name again and heard a faint cry. It was a magpie, he decided, for he saw one perched on the old clock tower.

He went back home and helped his mother and father with the papering until it was time for bed.

At school the next day, he looked for Roger to ask him what had happened. He could not see him.

'He's missing,' Walter Jones said.

'What do you mean?' Jack asked. At that moment Miss Cumberbatch called them into school. She seemed very serious and after prayers she told them that Roger had not been seen since tea-time yesterday.

'Have you seen him, Jack?' she said. 'You're his friend.'

Jack explained he had arranged to meet Roger but that he hadn't turned up.

'It's very worrying,' Miss Cumberbatch said. 'But I expect he'll be found.'

After school Jack went to Roger's house to ask if there was any news. Mr Marshall was very worried.

'Have you any idea where he might be?' Roger's father asked.

Jack hesitated. 'He wanders over the Downs,' he said at last. 'He says he knows his way about.'

'I thought so,' said Mr Marshall, shaking his head. 'I've told him over and over again.' He looked at Jack. 'You're not to blame, Jack. Don't look so guilty.'

'He was helping me make a rock collection,' Jack explained.

'The police have been searching the Downs. And I've been with them. But the place is honeycombed with shafts. We'll just have to keep on looking.'

He had come in from the search to get a flask of tea and to comfort Roger's mother. Mrs Marshall was a small, plump woman, who usually had a cheerful smile. But now she too was worried and anxious.

'He'll turn up safe and sound,' Mr

Marshall said to her. 'I'd better go back.'

'Can I come too?' Jack asked. He wanted to help. Roger was his friend.

'We'll call in to ask your mother. But if you come you must keep close by me and do exactly as you're told.'

'I will,' Jack said.

It was no use. The Downs went on for miles it seemed, and the search party had to move slowly and carefully. There were two police dogs which sniffed the ground and padded everywhere, but they didn't find anything.

When it became too dark to move safely the policeman in charge of the search said, 'We can't do any more now. Perhaps he's not on the Downs. Maybe he has run off somewhere.'

'He had no reason to run away,' Roger's father said.

'We'll give it another try at dawn tomorrow. There are plenty of people in the village who will help.'

The policemen went off, but Mr Marshall stayed for a while, calling into the night. Then he took hold of Jack's hand and together they walked away.

'We'll find him,' Jack said. 'I know we will.'

His mother made him go to school in the morning, though he would rather have joined in the search for his friend.

The morning passed without news. Everyone was quiet, even in the playground.

Towards the end of the afternoon Jack heard a whisper in his ear. 'What's the matter?'

It was Jenny. It was so long since he had seen her that he had forgotten all about her and he felt ashamed.

'It's Roger,' he said.

'Your friend.'

'He's missing. They think he might have fallen down a shaft.'

'Oh,' Jenny gave a long sigh and Jack thought she had gone again, but when he turned he could see her, her face streaked with dirt, as always.

She smiled and said. 'Don't worry. We'll find him.'

'We?'

'You and me.'

'When?'

'I'll come for you when I'm ready,' she said.

He saw Walter Jones staring at him but he didn't complain this time.

After school he went straight to Roger's house. Mrs Marshall answered the door. 'There's no news,' she said. 'They've given up searching the Downs. They think he must have gone off somewhere else.'

But Jack was sure Roger had fallen into a shaft while looking for rocks. He did not know why he felt so certain. He just knew. He wished he could go and look for his friend, even if everyone else had given up the search. But he knew it would not be safe. He tried to persuade his brother and sister to go, but they said it wasn't sensible. They said the search party had covered every inch of the area.

'He's not there, Jack. He can't be,' Roberta said.

Jack went to bed. He was still awake when Harry came to bed. They shared a room.

Harry said, 'Don't worry. I expect he's all right, hiding somewhere for a bit of fun.'

But it wasn't fun for anyone.

He could not get to sleep but Harry was soon snoring. Jack slipped out of bed and went to the window, staring out. He wished there was something he could do.

Someone was standing outside in the lane. It was Jenny. The moonlight shone through her, but he could see her plainly. She beckoned to him.

Harry was sound asleep. Jack crept past him and opened the bedroom door. The house was silent. Everyone must be in bed and asleep. He slowly went downstairs.

A sound above disturbed him. He heard footsteps and then the flush of the toilet. He crouched in the shadows,

but soon the cottage was quiet again, save for whisperings from his parents' room. Then they too were silent and he was able to move again.

He let himself out of the house and stood for a moment to get his breath. He was surprised how bright it was in the moonlight. He could see the path clearly in front of him, almost like daytime.

'Come on,' he heard Jenny's voice. 'I've not got long.'

He felt her hand on his arm drawing him in the direction of the Downs. His feet hardly seemed to touch the ground as they hurried along.

'I know where he'll be,' she said.

'Where?'

'Follow me.' She reached for his hand. 'Don't let go,' she said. 'You're safe as long as you stay with me.'

He did feel safe with Jenny.

'I know my way now,' she said. 'But I didn't. Once.'

He wanted to ask her more, find out all about her but she hurried on so quickly that in a moment they were in the centre of the Downs, near the old clock tower Roger had pointed out to him.

She stopped.

'Can't you hear?' she said.

He could hear nothing.

'Call him,' she said.

He called, 'Roger! Roger! Are you there?'

Silence.

He called again, 'Roger. It's me, Jack.'

Then he heard a sound, lost in the depths of the earth. It sounded like 'Jumping Jack, Jumping Jack, fell down a shaft and broke his back.'

'Roger,' he called. He was sure he had heard his friend. It *was* Roger.

'Jack,' a distant voice came back, then was silent again.

'I told you we'd find him,' Jenny said. 'I knew where he'd be.' She pulled him away. 'Come on. It's time to go.'

Jack did not want to leave. How could he leave his friend?

'Get help,' Jenny said. 'Get help.'

Help. Yes. That was what he must do. Get help. He turned to speak to Jenny but there was no Jenny. A cloud drifted over the moon and it was dark and he was alone at his bedroom window, looking out to the lane.

Chapter 11

He knew where Roger was. Jenny had
shown him. He must get help. He
went over to Harry and shook him.

'Wake up,' he said. 'Wake up.'

Harry sat up, startled at first, then
angry. 'What's up? Go to sleep.' He
lay down again and turned over.

'No, Harry. Wake up. Please. I
know where Roger is.'

Harry got out of bed and switched
the light on. He blinked and rubbed
the sleep from his eyes. He glared at
Jack. 'You'd better know what you're
saying. If you've got me out of bed

for nothing I'll crown you.'

'I know where he is. Honest.'

'Come on then, let's tell Dad. But he won't be pleased if you're wrong.'

'I know.'

Dad was quick to understand. 'But we can't do much till daylight,' he said. 'I'll go and tell Roger's father what you say. As soon as it's light enough to find our way over the Downs we'll go and look.'

Jack wanted to go there straightaway but Dad said it was too dangerous in the dark.

At dawn Mr Marshall, Dad and several other men gathered on the edge of the Downs.

'Where did you say he was?' Roger's father asked.

'By the clock tower,' Jack said. 'Down a shaft near there.' He was glad they didn't ask him how he knew. They wouldn't have believed his story about Jenny.

Mr Marshall looked at him as if he wondered how he was so certain.

'He told me he could find special rocks there.'

They picked their way carefully over to the clock tower.

'Here,' Jack said.

Mr Marshall stopped and cupped his hands round his mouth. 'Roger!' he called. 'Roger!' And, from somewhere near they heard a cry. 'Dad! Dad!'

'Thank God!' Mr Marshall said. 'Hold on, Roger. We'll get to you.'

The mouth of the shaft was behind the old tower, almost hidden by a heap of fallen stones.

'Careful,' said Mr Marshall as Jack hurried forward. 'We don't want to dislodge anything and have it fall down on top of him.' Slowly he began to lift stones from the rim of the shaft. He shone his powerful torch down.

'Dad!' Roger called, his voice sounding stronger.

'Can you see him?' Jack asked. 'Is he all right?'

Jack's father passed a rope to Mr

Marshall, who tied it round his waist. Slowly the men lowered him into the shaft.

'Hold it,' he called up after a while. 'I've got him. Heave ho!'

'Is he all right?' Jack shouted.

'Of course I am,' Roger answered. 'But I'm hungry.' His head appeared at the rim of the shaft, his face streaked with dirt and blood.

He clambered up and his father followed him. Roger staggered as he stood up and then sat on the ground.

'What is it?' said his father.

'I'm all right,' he said. He walked a few steps and then said, 'I'm a bit stiff.' His father gave him a piggy-back to Jack's house, which was nearest. Jack's mother and Mrs Marshall were waiting anxiously.

'There's not much wrong with him except a few cuts and bruises,' Mr Marshall said. 'But he might have been killed. Don't be so silly again, young man.'

'Leave him be,' Mrs Marshall said.

'He'll have learnt his lesson.'

But he could have been killed, Jack thought, as he looked at his friend, and saw his face. It reminded him of someone. It was Jenny, of course. Her face was scratched and dirty, as if she too had once tumbled down a shaft. And he remembered how he had seen her in the school room, covered in a blanket. He shuddered.

His mother was looking at him as if

she knew what he was thinking. 'Off to bed with you,' she said. 'No school for you this morning.'

He went upstairs but he couldn't sleep. He could hear voices downstairs as the search party congratulated themselves on finding Roger.

It was Jenny who had found him, not them. He and Jenny.

He went to his window, hoping to see her. But of course she was not there. He still could not sleep and looked for something to read to help him forget the excitement.

He saw the old newspaper they had found behind the fireplace and spread it on his bed. The edges were charred and the paper almost fell to pieces as he touched it. It was not like a modern newspaper. The printing was small and cramped. A headline caught his eye. 'Tragic Death of Girl. Fall Down Shaft'.

He caught his breath. There were gaps in the story where pieces of the paper had been burnt. 'A young girl,

newly arrived in the village of ...
dead at the bottom of a shaft ... clock
tower ... mine. The body was taken
to the school room ... few signs of
injury. The girl, Jenny Bryant ...
missing several days. A newcomer ...

without friends . . . nobody knew she was missing . . . found at last . . . too late to save her'.

'What's this?' Jack's mother put her head round the door. 'You should be sleeping.' She looked at him with concern. 'What's the matter, love? There's no need to cry. He's safe now.'

'Yes,' Jack said. '*He's* safe.'

'What do you mean?'

Jack shook his head. He could not explain, would never be able to explain.

In the afternoon he went to school, though he was tired from the night's doings. Everyone asked him what had happened, but he didn't want to talk about it.

He went to his desk and sat down, hoping Jenny would be there. But she wasn't. He tried to settle to work, but all the time he was thinking about Jenny. Poor Jenny, who had had no friends. But she had made friends with him, and with Mrs Pascoe. And with others too, perhaps. Maybe whenever strangers arrived she made them welcome.

'Jenny,' he whispered. 'I'll remember you.' He felt a breath at the back of his neck, the light touch of a hand on his and heard a chuckle. He looked up and saw the blackboard duster waving in the air, scattering clouds of chalk dust.

'Ashoo! Ashoo!' Miss Cumberbatch sneezed and the class suddenly burst out laughing.

THE END

A SELECTED LIST OF TITLES AVAILABLE
FROM YEARLING BOOKS

☐	862124	**SAM, THE GIRL DETECTIVE**	*Tony Bradman*	£2.50
☐	862744	**JULIAN, SECRET AGENT**	*Ann Cameron*	£2.50
☐	862094	**A DRAGON IN SPRING TERM**	*June Counsel*	£2.50
☐	862639	**ELLIE AND THE HAGWITCH**	*Helen Cresswell*	£2.50
☐	862167	**THE INTERGALACTIC OMNIGLOT**	*Jenni Fleetwood*	£1.99
☐	862612	**SCENT OF DANGER**	*Rosemary Hayes*	£1.99
☐	86285X	**CRAB**	*Anthony Masters*	£2.50
☐	862299	**SPRING-HEELED JACK**	*Philip Pullman*	£2.50
☐	862272	**ROOM 13**	*Robert Swindells*	£2.99
☐	862752	**THE POSTBOX MYSTERY**	*Robert Swindells*	£2.50
☐	862019	**THE CREATURE IN THE DARK**	*Robert Westall*	£2.50

*All Yearling Books are available at your bookshop or newsagent, or can be ordered from the
following address:*
Transworld Publishers Ltd,
Cash Sales Department,
PO Box 11, Falmouth, Cornwall TR10 9EN

Please send a cheque or postal order, (no currency) and allow £1.00 for postage and packing for
one book, an additional 50p for a second book, and an additional 30p for each subsequent book
ordered to a maximum charge of £3.00 if ordering seven or more books.

Overseas customers, including Eire, please allow £2.00 for postage and packing for the first book,
an additional £1.00 for a second book, and an additional 50p for each subsequent title ordered.

NAME (Block Letters) ....

ADDRESS ....

....

We hope you enjoyed reading this book. If you would like to receive details of the latest new
children's books published by Transworld Publishers, please send your name and address to: The
Children's Books Editor, Transworld Publishers Ltd, 61-63 Uxbridge Road, Ealing, London W5
5SA, marking your envelope CHILDREN'S NEWSLETTER.